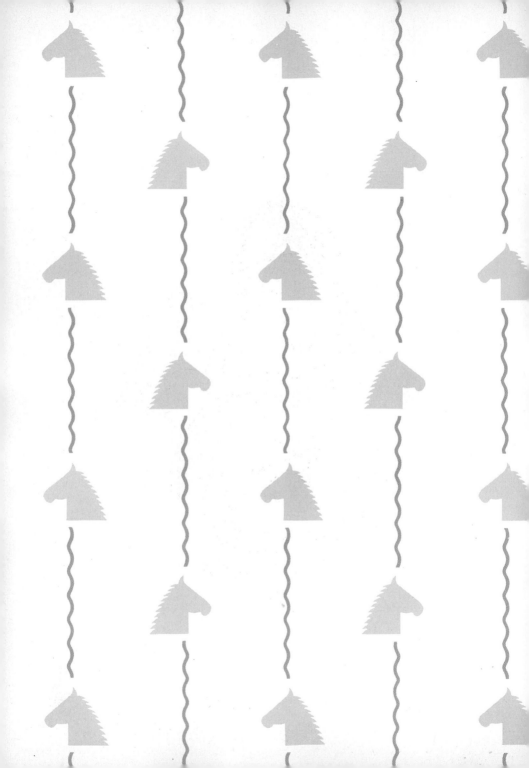

The
GOOD LUCK PONY

Story and Pictures

by

Elizabeth Koda-Callan

WORKMAN PUBLISHING, NEW YORK

Published simultaneously in Canada
by Thomas Allen & Son Limited.

Library of Congress Cataloging-in-Publication Data

Koda-Callan, Elizabeth.
The good luck pony / by Elizabeth Koda-Callan.
p. cm.
Summary: A little girl finds the courage to ride when her mother
gives her a tiny golden pony that radiates self-confidence.
ISBN 0-89480-859-1
[1. Self-confidence — Fiction. 2. Horsemanship — Fiction.]
1. Title   90-50366
PZ7.K8175Go 1990   CIP
[E] — dc20   AC

Workman Publishing Company
708 Broadway
New York, New York 10003
Printed in Hong Kong
First Printing
10 9 8 7 6 5 4 3 2 1

For Carol Devine Carson

and

Jennifer and Chelsea

Once there was a little girl who loved horses. She admired their smooth, silky coats and fine, strong bodies. She hoped that someday she would ride a real one.

Before long the little girl began
taking riding lessons. The first thing she

learned was how to mount a pony and
how to use the reins to guide him.

Once a week for several weeks she walked her pony around a ring with three other girls.

The ponies moved quite slowly, but the little girl dreamed of riding as fast as the wind.

One day the little girl was assigned a new pony. He was much friskier than the one she had been riding. The little girl felt uneasy on this pony. As the class walked the ponies from the stable to the ring, the little girl became more unsure of herself. Suddenly, the pony took off with the little girl bouncing stiffly in the saddle. The little girl had dropped the reins, but she held on tightly to the pony's mane. The pony headed for the trail as tree branches whipped by the little girl's face. She was very frightened.

The instructor saw that the pony was out of control, and she set off after him. Within a few moments the instructor reached the little girl's side and grabbed the pony's reins. The pony whinnied and came to a halt. By the time the little girl and her instructor returned to the class, the little girl was scratched and very shaken.

At the stable, the little girl's mother was waiting. She cleaned the scratches on the little girl's face and hands.

"I don't *ever* want to get on a horse again," the little girl said, trying to hold back tears.

"That must have been quite a scare for you," her mother said softly. She put her arm around the little girl. "I know how much you've dreamed of being able to ride. You just need to give yourself a chance to feel comfortable on a pony. It may take time and patience to learn something new, but I know you can do it if you keep at it."

The little girl thought about her dream of riding a horse. She had expected it would be much quicker and easier to learn than it was. It was all very confusing. She still dreamed of riding, but she was afraid just *thinking* about getting back on a pony.

The following week, on the day of her riding lesson, the little girl panicked. "I don't feel like going to the class today," she told her mother.

"I think I have something that will help you with your riding," her mother said. She handed the little girl a small flannel pouch. The little girl opened it and pulled out a tiny golden horse charm on a golden chain.

"This lucky necklace will help you get back on a horse and ride the way you would like to . . . if you believe in it," said the little girl's mother. "But you must act on your dream to make it lucky."

The little girl put on the necklace. The golden horse gleamed in the afternoon light. She called it her "Good Luck Pony."

The little girl wore the Good Luck Pony to the riding class that afternoon. Still, when she saw the pony that she was assigned, her heart started beating faster. The instructor realized she was afraid. "There are some exercises you can do that will make you feel more comfortable on the pony," she said. "These exercises will help you develop confidence and balance. Your pony ran away because he sensed you were afraid and had forgotten how to control him. But if you continue to practice the commands and do the exercises, you will feel more confident and you will be able to get the pony to do what you want him to do."

The little girl was still uncertain, but she agreed to do the exercises if the pony stood still. While the instructor held the horse's reins, the little girl did the exercises.

First, she learned to sit balanced in the saddle.

Then she reached forward and patted her pony's neck.

She leaned back and patted him on the rump.

She practiced turning in the saddle, first with her hands on her hips and then with her arms extended outward.

With her right hand, she reached down and touched her toes. Then she did the same with her left hand. And every time she did these exercises she wore the Good Luck Pony necklace.

After bending and stretching, lean-
ing forward and back, she began to feel
more comfortable on the pony.

Weeks passed, and the little girl discovered how to control her pony by using her hands, legs, and body weight. The pony became comfortable with her commands and she became good at guiding him and making him move exactly where she wanted him to go. She learned to trot and even canter. The Good Luck Pony was certainly bringing her good luck.

In the months that followed, she continued to exercise and practice. She had almost forgotten her fear until one day the instructor told the class that they were going to learn how to jump. The little girl had always dreamed of jumping, but she was afraid of actually having to do it.

The little girl watched her classmates. They seemed to be making their jumps with ease. Suddenly, she had that same heart-pounding feeling she had had when she was on the runaway pony. She could barely hear. her instructor's voice, which now seemed small and distant next to the loud pounding of her heart. "The Good Luck Pony can't help me this time," she thought.

Yet she found herself looking at the golden charm that hung around her neck. She thought about how she had worn her Good Luck Pony through all of her exercises and practice sessions. And how she had mastered so many of the commands that at first appeared so difficult. "Maybe my Good Luck Pony *is* lucky," she thought. "It helps me to remember all the exercises and commands that I now know I can do. When I think of this, I'm less afraid."

She took a deep breath as she walked her pony to the low rail. She was a bit unbalanced as the pony stepped over it. Next she guided him through at a trot, and then at a canter. Over a slightly higher rail, he finally jumped. And what a jump! It was much bigger than she expected. Her pounding heart seemed to stop as she rode the pony over the rail. But she stayed with him. And she kept her balance.

Her instructor and classmates cheered. The little girl beamed with happiness.

After class, they all went out to celebrate with ice-cream sodas. "You were determined and stuck with it. That was what brought you good luck," said her instructor.

From then on, the little girl wore the Good Luck Pony every time she went riding. The Good Luck Pony was indeed lucky. It reminded her that it was her own effort that brought her good luck. And from that day on she never forgot it.

About the Author

Elizabeth Koda-Callan grew up in Connecticut and now lives in New York City with her daughter, Jennifer, and their cat, Cinnamon. She is the creator of the well-loved children's books THE MAGIC LOCKET and THE SILVER SLIPPERS.

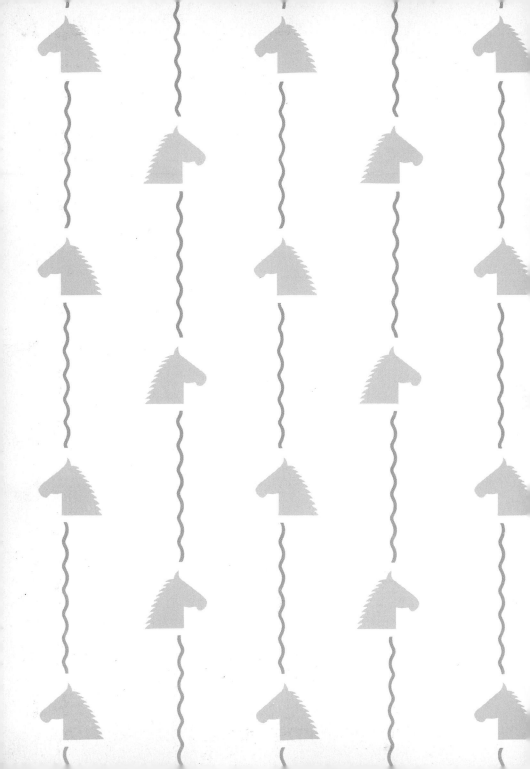